MR. CHRISTMAS

by Roger Hargreaves

Illustrated by
Adam Hargreaves

EGMONT

In my snow-covered cottage at the South Pole I was having breakfast.

Christmas Pudding!

That frosty morning, as I was popping the last piece of marmalade-covered plum pudding into my mouth, there was a knock on the door of Mistletoe Cottage.

When I opened the door, I saw that it was the postman.

Mistletoe
Cottage

"Hello, Percy," I said. "Come on in out of the cold."

"Don't mind if I do," replied Percy. "There's a bit of a nip in the air today."

"I've got a letter for you," said Percy. "And as it has a North Pole postmark, I suppose it's from your uncle."

Everybody at the South Pole knows about my famous uncle who lives at the North Pole.

"Good old Father Christmas," I chuckled. "Haven't heard from him for ages!"

"Well," remarked Percy, "thanks for the warm-up. I had better be off now."

I opened the envelope.

"Dear Nephew," read the letter, "I hope all is well down there. We are busy as usual up here, getting things organised for Christmas. Which is one of the reasons I am writing to you.

"Can you help?

"Each year I am finding it more and more difficult to get round all those Mr. Men! There seem to be so many of them all over the place, and I was wondering if, this year, as a big favour to your old uncle, you could stand in for me?

"Hoping you can help. Your ever loving uncle."

That very evening I put through a long distance call to North Pole 253.

"Hello?" chuckled a rather deep, rumbly voice at the other end of the telephone, "Father Christmas speaking!"

"Hello Uncle," I said. "Your letter arrived this morning, and I'd love to help!"

"Oh good for you," the voice rumbled in my ear. "If you have a pencil and paper, I'll give you the Mr Men's names and addresses."

"I'd no idea there were so many of them," I said.

"Do you think you can manage?" asked my famous uncle. "I'll lend you a couple of reindeer if you like."

"Oh no," I said. "I can manage."

I read through the list of Mr. Men while I was having supper.

"This is going to keep me busy," I said. "First things first," I thought to myself. "And the first thing I need is transport!"

"And the first thing to do if I need transport," I thought as I chewed, "is to talk to the Wizard!"

Wizard Winterbottom!

The following morning, I set off to see the Wizard.

It had been snowing again during the night, and I was quite out of breath by the time I arrived at Wizard Winterbottom's castle.

I must say it's the biggest castle I've ever seen.

Mind you, it has to be big, because Wizard Winterbottom is a giant.

And there, goodness knows how many times taller than me, stood the huge figure of Wizard Winterbottom.

"Christmas!" he boomed in a voice that made my head spin. "How nice to see you! Come in! Follow me!"

"Now," thundered Wizard Winterbottom. "What brings you here on a cold winter's morning like this?"

I told him all about my famous uncle, and all about how I'd been asked to help, and all about the Mr Men, and all about where they lived, and all about the fact that I needed transport. Special transport!

"Humph!" retorted the Wizard.

"Can you help me?" I asked hopefully.

"Yes," he said eventually. "But I can't do anything until the middle of next week!"

"Thank you very much," I replied.

"Goodbye!" I shouted, but he didn't hear me, he was already too busy thinking.

Exactly two weeks later I paid a return visit to the enormous castle.

"Hello, Christmas," boomed the giant voice.

He took me into his kitchen, lifted me up on to his enormous table, and set me down with a bit of a bump.

"There's your transport," said Wizard Winterbottom.

"But that's your teapot!" I said in bewilderment.

"You've heard of flying saucers," he laughed. "Well, you're looking at the world's first flying teapot!"

"Gosh," I said. "How does it work?"

"Teabags," came the thunderous reply. "I've put an engine inside the spout! All you do is refuel every thousand miles, and you can fly at up to three times the speed of sound!"

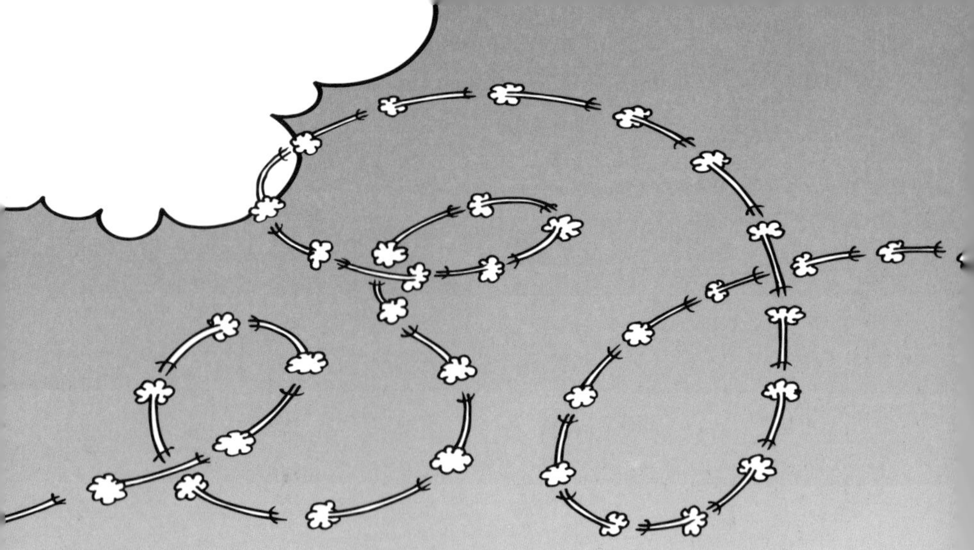

We took the Flying Teapot outside the castle, and I pressed the start button in great excitement.

I zoomed right around the South Pole in no time at all, and landed safely back at the castle.

"Well?" asked Wizard Winterbottom.

I was lost for words.

"Fanjollytastic?" suggested the wizard.

I grinned. "Absojollylutely," I replied.

That evening, I sat down and made a list of Christmas presents for all the Mr Men.

Another list.

A very long list.

I didn't finish until three o'clock in the morning!

I spent the next week and a half wrapping up all the presents, and almost before I knew it, December 24th arrived.

Christmas Eve!

"It's going to be a long day," I thought to myself as I packed all the brightly coloured parcels into my Flying Teapot.

It was snowing lightly as I took off from the South Pole.

That Christmas Eve was indeed a very long day, and a very long night too.

And the moon was just disappearing over the horizon of Loudland when I delivered the last of the presents to Mr. Quiet.

I was quite exhausted.

Christmas morning dawned, and all over the world everyone started to open their presents.

At seven o'clock Mr Fussy opened his present.
Three hundred and sixty five yellow dusters.
One for every day of the year!

At five past seven Mr Small opened his present.
One jelly bean! Gift wrapped. Banana flavoured.
A feast!

At ten past seven Mr Greedy opened his present.
A cookery book entitled: 1001 ways to roast an ox!
Mr Greedy licked his lips and rubbed his tummy.

At quarter past seven Mr Tall opened his present. Socks. Striped socks. The longest, stripiest pair of stretchy socks you've ever seen!

At twenty past seven Mr Muddle opened a packet of cornflakes.
"Funny sort of present," he thought to himself, not noticing his real present.

At twenty-five past seven Mr Mean opened his present. A purse. A very, very small purse. Just small enough not to take any money!

At half past seven Mr Forgetful opened his present.
"Is it my birthday?" he thought to himself.

At twenty to eight Mr Chatterbox opened his present.
A dictionary.
"How very very very very very very very very useful," he murmured.

At a quarter to eight Mr Topsy-Turvy opened his present. A picture.
"How nice," he said as he hung it on the wall.
Upside down!

At ten to eight Mr Uppity opened his present.
A present for the man who has everything.
A gold-plated backscratcher!

At five to eight Mr Funny opened his present.
A book of knock knock jokes.
Knock-knock! Who's there? You know the sort of thing.

And, at eight o'clock precisely, Mr Silly opened his present.
An electric, fully automatic, instant, digital, computerised Thingumajig!

What's an electric, fully automatic, instant, digital, computerised Thingumajig?

I've no idea!

Just after eight o'clock that Christmas morning the telephone rang.

"Hello," rumbled a voice.

"Hello," I answered. "Happy Christmas!"

"That's me," laughed Father Christmas. "And a happy Christmas to you too."

"And that's me too," I replied.

"How did it go?" Father Christmas asked me.

"Just got back," I said.

"Me too," sighed my uncle wearily. "Had a bit of a problem in France," he added. "Got stuck in a chimney."

"It's all those mince pies," I chuckled.

And that is the end of my story.

Well.

Nearly.

Almost.

Not quite.

At five o'clock in the afternoon Mr Slow finally managed to open his present.

Five o'clock in the afternoon was the time.

And the day?

New Year's Eve!

CUT ALONG DOTTED LINE AND RETURN THIS WHOLE PAGE

3 Great Offers for MR.MEN Fans!

1 New Mr. Men or Little Miss Library Bus Presentation Cases

A brand new stronger, roomier school bus library box, with sturdy carrying handle and stay-closed fasteners.
The full colour, wipe-clean boxes make a great home for your full collection.
They're just £5.99 inc P&P and free bookmark!

☐ MR. MEN ☐ LITTLE MISS (please tick and order overleaf)

2 Door Hangers and Posters

In every Mr. Men and Little Miss book like this one, you will find a special token. Collect 6 tokens and we will send you a brilliant Mr. Men or Little Miss poster and a Mr. Men or Little Miss double sided full colour bedroom door hanger of your choice. Simply tick your choice in the list and tape a 50p coin for your two items to this page.

Door Hangers (please tick)

- ☐ Mr. Nosey & Mr. Muddle
- ☐ Mr. Slow & Mr. Busy
- ☐ Mr. Messy & Mr. Quiet
- ☐ Mr. Perfect & Mr. Forgetful
- ☐ Little Miss Fun & Little Miss Late
- ☐ Little Miss Helpful & Little Miss Tidy
- ☐ Little Miss Busy & Little Miss Brainy
- ☐ Little Miss Star & Little Miss Fun

Posters (please tick)

- ☐ MR.MEN
- ☐ LITTLE MISS

PLEASE STICK YOUR 50P COIN HERE

3 Sixteen Beautiful Fridge Magnets – any 2 for £2.00! inc.P&P

They're very special collector's items!
Simply tick your first and second* choices from the list below of any 2 characters!

1st Choice

- ☐ Mr. Happy
- ☐ Mr. Lazy
- ☐ Mr. Topsy-Turvy
- ☐ Mr. Bounce
- ☐ Mr. Bump
- ☐ Mr. Small
- ☐ Mr. Snow
- ☐ Mr. Wrong
- ☐ Mr. Daydream
- ☐ Mr. Tickle
- ☐ Mr. Greedy
- ☐ Mr. Funny
- ☐ Little Miss Giggles
- ☐ Little Miss Splendid
- ☐ Little Miss Naughty
- ☐ Little Miss Sunshine

2nd Choice

- ☐ Mr. Happy
- ☐ Mr. Lazy
- ☐ Mr. Topsy-Turvy
- ☐ Mr. Bounce
- ☐ Mr. Bump
- ☐ Mr. Small
- ☐ Mr. Snow
- ☐ Mr. Wrong
- ☐ Mr. Daydream
- ☐ Mr. Tickle
- ☐ Mr. Greedy
- ☐ Mr. Funny
- ☐ Little Miss Giggles
- ☐ Little Miss Splendid
- ☐ Little Miss Naughty
- ☐ Little Miss Sunshine

*Only in case your first choice is out of stock.

TO BE COMPLETED BY AN ADULT

To apply for any of these great offers, ask an adult to complete the coupon below and send it with the appropriate payment and tokens, if needed, to MR. MEN OFFERS, PO BOX 7, MANCHESTER M19 2HD

☐ Please send ____ Mr. Men Library case(s) and/or ____ Little Miss Library case(s) at £5.99 each inc P&P

☐ Please send a poster and door hanger as selected overleaf. I enclose six tokens plus a 50p coin for P&P

☐ Please send me ____ pair(s) of Mr. Men/Little Miss fridge magnets, as selected above at £2.00 inc P&P

Fan's Name ____________________

Address ____________________

____________________ **Postcode** ____________

Date of Birth ____________________

Name of Parent/Guardian ____________________

Total amount enclosed £____________

☐ **I enclose a cheque/postal order payable to Egmont Books Limited**

☐ **Please charge my MasterCard/Visa/Amex/Switch or Delta account** (delete as appropriate)

																		Card Number

Expiry date __/__ **Signature** ____________________

Please allow 28 days for delivery. Offer is only available while stocks last. We reserve the right to change the terms of this offer at any time and we offer a 14 day money back guarantee. This does not affect your statutory rights. Data Protection Act: If you do not wish to receive other similar offers from us or companies we recommend, please tick this box ☐. Offers apply to UK only.

MR.MEN LITTLE MISS

CUT ALONG DOTTED LINE AND RETURN THIS WHOLE PAGE